The Best Friends Club

A Lizzie and Harold Story

By Elizabeth Winthrop • Pictures by Martha Weston

HARCOURT BRACE & COMPANY

Orlando Atlanta Austin Boston San Francisco Chicago Dallas New York
Toronto London

This edition is published by special arrangement with Lothrop, Lee & Shepard Books, a division of William Morrow & Company, Inc.

Grateful acknowledgment is made to Lothrop, Lee & Shepard Books, a division of William Morrow & Company, Inc. for permission to reprint The Best Friends Club *by Elizabeth Winthrop, illustrated by Martha Weston.*

Printed in the United States of America

ISBN 0-15-303636-2

4 5 6 7 8 9 10 060 97 96

To Natalie and Katharine and Stewart,
three good friends
E.W.
To Jude
M.W.

Lizzie and Harold were best friends.

Harold taught Lizzie how to do cat's cradle.

Lizzie taught Harold how to play running bases.

Lizzie shared her trick-or-treat candy with Harold, and Harold let Lizzie ride his big red bike.

They always walked home from school together.

“Let’s start a best friends club,” Lizzie said one day.
“Great,” said Harold. “We can meet under your porch. That will be our clubhouse.”

Harold painted the sign.
It said
THE BF CLUB.

"Now write *Members Only*," said Lizzie.

"You write it," said Harold. "My teacher says my M's are too fat."

So Lizzie wrote *Members Only.*

"Who are the members?" Harold asked.

"You and me," said Lizzie.

"That's all?"

"Yes," said Lizzie. "You can be the president and I'll be the vice-president. The president gets to write down all the rules."

"You be the president," Harold said. "Your writing is better than mine."

"All right, then I'll be president," said Lizzie. "Now we'll make up the rules."

"Rule number one," said Harold. "The club meets under Lizzie's porch."

"Right," said Lizzie. "Rule number two. Nobody else can be in the club."

"Rule number three," said Harold. He thought for a long time. "I can't think of any more."

"Rule number three," said Lizzie. "Lizzie and Harold walk home from school together every day."

"Rule number four," said Harold. "Everybody in the club knows cat's cradle."

THE BF CLUB
Members only
Rules
1. The club meets
under Lizzie's
porch.
2. Nobody

They heard voices. Someone was walking by. They could see two pairs of feet.

"It's Christina," whispered Lizzie. "She always wears those black party shoes."

"And Douglas," Harold whispered back. "His shoelaces are always untied."

"I'm only having Nancy and Amy and Stacey to my birthday party," they heard Christina say.

"My mother said I could have my whole class," Douglas answered. "We're going to play baseball."

"Oh goody," said Harold. "That means I'll be invited to Douglas's birthday party."

"I won't," Lizzie said gloomily. She was in a different class.

The next day, Harold came out of his classroom with Douglas.

"He wants to walk home with us," Harold said to Lizzie.

"He can't," said Lizzie.

"Why not?" asked Harold.

"Harold, remember the rules. We're best friends and we always walk home together," Lizzie said. "Just you and me."

"Oh yeah," said Harold. "I forgot."

Douglas looked very sad.

"Sorry, Douglas," Harold said. "See you tomorrow."

"Douglas's ears stick out," Lizzie said on the way home.

"So what?" said Harold.

"His shoelaces are always dripping," said Lizzie.

"I don't care about that," said Harold.

"I'll meet you in the clubhouse after snacks," said Lizzie.

"I can't come today," said Harold. "My mother wants me home."

Lizzie sat in the clubhouse all by herself.

She wrote down more rules.

They said

5. Best friends don't go to other people's birthday parties.

6. People with funny ears and drippy shoelaces are not allowed in the club.

The next day, Harold came out of his classroom with Douglas again.

"Douglas asked me to play at his house," said Harold.

"*Harold*," said Lizzie. "What about the club?"

"What club?" asked Douglas.

"None of your business," said Lizzie.

"I'll come tomorrow," said Harold. "I promise."

Lizzie watched them walk away together. She stuck out her tongue at them but Harold didn't turn around.

She went straight to the clubhouse and wrote down another rule. It said

7. Best friends don't go to other people's houses to play.

Then she threw a ball at the garage wall until suppertime.

"Douglas wants to be in the club," said Harold the next day.

"He can't be," said Lizzie. "Only best friends are allowed in this club."

She showed him all the new rules she had written down.

"This club is no fun," said Harold. "It has too many rules. I quit."

He crawled out from under the porch and walked home.

Lizzie took down his sign and put up a new one.

Douglas came down the street.

He was riding Harold's new bicycle.

Harold was chasing after him.

When Harold saw the sign, he stopped and read it.

"What does it say?" asked Douglas.

"It says, 'Lizzie's Club. Nobody Else Allowed,' " Harold said.

LIZZIE'S
CLUB
NOBody Else
Allowed.

Harold leaned over and looked at Lizzie. "You can't have a club with only one person," he said.

"*I* can," said Lizzie.

"A three-person club is more fun," said Harold. "Douglas knows how to do cat's cradle."

"But he's not a best friend," said Lizzie.

"It'll be a different kind of club," said Harold. "We'll make up a new name."

"Maybe," said Lizzie.

She sat under the porch and watched them.
First they played bicycle tag.
Then they threw the ball at her garage wall.

"Want to play running bases?" Lizzie asked.

"I don't know how," said Douglas.

"I'll teach you," said Lizzie.

They took turns being the runner. Lizzie was the fastest.

AFTER THREE TAGS, A RUNNER TRADES PLACES WITH THE CATCHER WHO MADE THE LAST TAG.
Gotcha!
NOW GO BACK TO THE FIRST STEP.
That's one!
(REMEMBER THIS IS USUALLY A GROUP OF KIDS, SO IT'S EASIER TO TAG SOMEONE.)
...and easier to get away.
THE GAME IS OVER WHEN EVERYONE HAS HAD ENOUGH.

Douglas whispered something to Harold.

"Douglas wants you to come to his birthday party," said Harold.

Then Lizzie whispered something to Harold.

"Lizzie says yes," Harold said to Douglas.

"And I've thought of a new name for the club," said Lizzie. "Douglas can be in it too."

"Oh boy!" said Douglas.

"You can be the first member. I am the president and Harold is the vice-president," said Lizzie.

"That's okay with me," said Harold.

"Me too," said Douglas.

It was getting dark.

Douglas went home for supper.

Lizzie crawled back under the porch. She tore up her sign and her list of rules.

"What's the new name for the club?" Harold asked.

"I'll show you," said Lizzie.

She sat down and wrote in great big letters

THE NO RULES CLUB.

Harold smiled.

He stuck up the sign with a thumbtack.

Then they both went upstairs to Lizzie's house for supper.